Dear reader,

This book is based on fictional characters developed by my son, Jackson Stegall, and myself. All character traits and names developed purely from our imagination as we would craft bedtime stories about the obstacles and triumphs of a fictional character named Marvin Migelroy. Any resemblance to actual people is completely coincidental.

We hope you enjoy it!

—Daron Stegall

A *Higher Purpose Living* Publication

HigherPurposeLiving.com

TEXT DESIGN BY ASHLEY MUEHLBAUER

The MOSTLY UNFORTUNATE Misadventures of Marvin Migelroy

→ MARVIN *HITS* THE POOL ←

DARON STEGALL AND JACKSON STEGALL

Illustrated by Johanna van der Sterre

→ CONTENTS ←

^G Marvin has his own glossary! If you see an awkward little G next to a word, you can find that word in the glossary to see what it means. For example:

AWKWARD Something that doesn't look quite right or move quite right. Maybe it's a little too big or small or doesn't seem to fit at all. Sometimes Marvin is a little awkward - well, or REALLY awkward. It doesn't mean he's not cool. He's just different. Read on, you'll see what I mean!

To grandma and grandpa and the rest of our awesome, amazing, fun family . . . you know who you are. Don't make me call you out.

GRANDPA   GRANDMA

→ CHAPTER 1 ←
A TERRIFYING EXPERIENCE

"Are you excited?" Marvin's mom asked as they were hurriedly^G trying to get out of the house.

"Nerrr-Nervous is more like it" Marvin responded with a slight quiver in his voice. He felt like he had a swarm of butterflies dancing around in his stomach.

"Nervous?" his mom asked. She was a little confused. "You're a good swimmer. I don't think you have anything to be nervous about."

"Mom! In case you don't remember, I was the only one in swim class who immediately sank to the bottom like a stone!" exclaimed Marvin. "AND I had followed *every* step the instructor taught us," he continued while recalling the terrifying swim lesson experiences from years ago.

"Yeah, that's true. You did follow the instructions to the letter. And you still sank like a rock," said Marvin's mom. She held back a little smile as she remembered Marvin's earliest swim lessons.

Back then, it had been tough for Marvin's mom to watch her son struggle. Now, years later, she could finally look back and reflect on how cute her son had looked as he kicked his scrawny little arms and legs while trying to stay afloat.

"Marvin, that was several years ago. Last year, if I remember correctly, you were a doggy-paddling sensation!" She was still poking fun at Marvin, but she was also trying

3

to put a positive twist on something she knew was a traumatic experience for her son.

Truth was, Marvin was a pretty strong swimmer nowadays, so it wasn't the swimming he was worried about. He wasn't even worried about the infamous corkscrew waterslide that the local kids had dubbed *The Slip and Skid* because of the skin-stripping dry spots along its path. It was something much scarier than either of these—something he wanted to conquer so badly but wouldn't dare take the chance.

The chance of embarrassment, the chance of everlasting harassment, the chance of injury or worse yet! . . . the chance of . . . well, you get the idea.

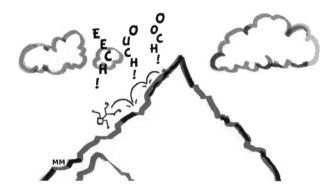

Marvin had stopped walking toward the car and was just standing there in the driveway, frozen, thinking about his fate when his mom snapped him back to reality.

"Let's go Marvin! You're going to be late for the party," she shouted through the open car window.

The party Marvin's mom was referring to was for none other than Lindsay Sutton, a new girl who had just transferred to his school.

Lindsay was a little taller, a little faster and a little smarter than most of the other kids in her grade. On the playground, she was almost impossible to catch in a game of tag. In the classroom, she rarely missed an answer.

More importantly, however, Lindsay was also very kind to everyone and the first one to lend a hand if a fellow student was struggling. Teachers and students all seemed to think she was a pretty awesome kid.

If you asked Marvin what he thought of Lindsay, he would say that she was the smartest girl in his class. What he might not tell you is that he also thought she was the prettiest girl in the school.

→ CHAPTER 2 ←
WHAT IS IT?

As they arrived at the Keller Pointe Pool and Recreational Center, Marvin couldn't help but notice "IT" looming^G in the distance.

"IT" must have been at least one hundred feet high.

From the parking lot, he could already hear the screams of some of the older kids as they plunged^G off its edge in terror and plummeted^G toward the water below.

"Aiieeeeeee," he heard echoing from behind the trees.

These weren't just any screams. They seemed to gain a new level of shrillness and volume as they progressed, and they lasted for what seemed like forever. "Aiieeeeeeeee," he heard again off in the distance.

"Maybe this party isn't such a great idea," said Marvin.

"What? You're changing your mind now?" asked his mom confused by Marvin's crazy talk. "You really like this girl. You love to swim. She was nice enough to invite you. There's no backing out now. You are definitely going in."

With a few more words of encouragement, and a little push, they both entered the pool area where they were quickly greeted by Lindsay's mom. "Marvin!" she exclaimed from the pool steps happy to see him, "We're so glad you made it!"

"Me too, Mrs. Sutton, thank you for inviting me," Marvin responded in a low mumbling voice while he was thinking to himself, *How am I going to get out of this mess?*

"Well, have a great time," Marvin's mom said after giving him a peck on his head and

quickly turning to leave. She knew she had better get out of there fast before her son changed his mind. "I'll pick you up in three hours. Be sure to keep your hat on when you're not in the water. You know how fast your cute little cheeky weekys burn," she yelled over her shoulder while walking toward the exit.

Well, that was seriously embarrassing, Marvin thought. He was horrified that his mom had just said that out loud.

"Yeah, okay, Mom," Marvin quickly replied, hoping his mother wasn't about to blurt out another *helpful* suggestion.

Marvin tested the pool water with the toes on his left foot. Yikes!! It wasn't just cold, it was FREEZING!

There's no way I'm getting into that water, he thought.

Just then, he heard Lindsay holler, "Jump in Marvin! It's not cold!" She was hanging out in the middle of the pool with a few of their classmates.

And just like that, *freezing* no longer mattered. Marvin leaped off the edge with no fear and no hesitation.

But, there was one big problem. His hat was still on! Marvin realized it in midair and at the last second made a fumbling attempt to toss it from his head onto the pool deck.

But he missed.

At least he missed the pool deck. He did manage to peg the lifeguard squarely in the eyes. The sharp blow of Marvin's hat brim knocked him off the edge of the pool where he was perched ready to save sinking kids.

Marvin popped to the water's surface to see the results of his ninja-like, midair hat toss only to discover the harsh reality of his throwing skills.

He almost felt like going under the water again because not only was he surrounded by a bunch of kids laughing their heads off, but also one seriously wet and angry lifeguard.

"Thanks a lot for nailing me in the head, kid! I should confiscate[G] that hat. It's a lethal weapon," the lifeguard said firmly as he hoisted himself up out of the water back to his poolside perch.

"Oops! Sorry!" Marvin said as the laughing heads bobbed around him in the water. Surprisingly, his favorite black hat had survived the incident. It was sitting at the pool's edge safe and dry.

→ CHAPTER 3 ←
PARTY CRASHER

After swimming a few laps to warm himself up and shake off his jitters, Marvin decided he had better get his beach towel, Lindsay's gift, and his favorite black hat over to the birthday table before something else went wrong.

At the birthday area, Marvin realized he had arrived just in time—*Just in cake-and-ice cream time!*

If Marvin was good at anything it was eating cake and ice cream.

"May I please have the end piece with extra icing?" Marvin asked. Without hesitation, one of the moms who was serving handed him a huge, white frosting-covered piece of chocolate cake with red, white and blue confetti sprinkles AND 2 big scoops of vanilla bean ice-cream. "Sweeeet! Thanks a lot!" Marvin exclaimed as he grabbed a white plastic fork off the table and got ready to dig in.

As Marvin stood confidently under the red and blue umbrella devouring his big chunk of cake, he gazed across the pool and noticed a few of his classmates were still out in the water, including Lindsay who was waving at him. He could tell she was saying something to him but couldn't make out the words.

"Hey, Lindsay!" Marvin shouted while waving his fork in the air. "Awesome cake!" he yelled before continuing to scarf down the delicious treat.

Lindsay continued shouting and waving and Marvin continued waving and eating.

And then it hit him. *Shouldn't Lindsay be here at the table eating her birthday cake now?*

"Marvin! You are at the wrong table!" he faintly heard Lindsay saying as she swam past the screaming and splashing kids.

And then it REALLY hit him. *Ohhhhhhhh Nooooooo!* Marvin thought. *I am at the wrong birthday party!*

In what seemed like slow motion, Marvin turned back to look at the table behind him. He didn't recognize a single person, not the moms, not the kids, *not a soul!*

He was so excited about diving into the cake that it didn't occur to him there could be more than one birthday party going on at the Keller Pointe Recreational Center! And to make matters worse, he hadn't even noticed that the kids at this table were probably a good three years younger than him. Basically, Marvin had just crashed a little kid's birthday party and stolen some of their cake and ice cream.

That mom probably thought I was one of the big brothers or something, Marvin thought, as he quickly pulled his hat down low over his

eyes, snatched up his items and followed the hand gesture of Lindsay pointing toward the opposite end of the pool.

"Got it!" he hollered back casually. He wished she hadn't seen the entire embarrassing scene unfold.

Pull it together Marvin, he thought as he crept over to the proper table while trying not to draw more attention to himself.

"Hey, Marvin. You're just in time! I was about to call everybody out of the water for cake and ice cream!" Lindsay's mom said as Marvin arrived at the right birthday table.

"Oh, great," Marvin muttered as he stood there with a bellyful of cake and a bright red face from the embarrassment of his birthday party invasion mishap.

"Marvin, here's a piece of chocolate cake with extra icing and a big scoop of ice cream just for you," said Lindsay's mother as she pushed it across the table toward him.

"I'll take that one, Mom," a voice said out of nowhere. "Marvin and I will just share," said Lindsay giving a wink to Marvin.

Wow! That was cool! Marvin thought. *Lindsay was totally looking out for me and probably saved my stomach from exploding!*

→ CHAPTER 4 ←
THE OTHER
PARTY CRASHER

As the kids were finishing their cake and Lindsay was about to open her gifts, Marvin stood close to her just in case she needed any help or some extra muscle to break open a stubborn box.

Everything was going just swimmingly^C, well, that was until Marvin heard the one voice that instantly put a sinking feeling into his stomach.

"What's up Migel-worm?" the voice said in its traditional intimidating^C tone.

There he stood, the last person Marvin ever expected to see at Lindsay Sutton's birthday party. It was Beau Bradley. There was no way Lindsay would have invited him which meant just one thing. Beau Bradley had crashed the party.

Most of the kids called Beau Bradley *Bo-Bo* for short, behind his back, of course. But that cute nickname didn't fool anyone. There wasn't anything cute about Bo-Bo.

Bo-Bo was a big kid with a quick temper. Rumor had it that he had once flipped his mom's car over on its side just because she had *suggested* he clean his room!

"What are you doing here, Beau?" Lindsay snapped, as she tried to diffuse[G] the situation before Beau Bradley got out of hand. She had seen that happen many times before.

"Just stopping by to see how the party is going," Beau responded. "What do you think of that high-dive, Marvin?" he continued, as he wasted no time trying to get under Marvin's skin.

"I don't think anything about it," Marvin responded in a calm, almost stoic^G, voice.

"I dare you to jump off of it," said Bo-Bo loud enough so that everyone at the table would hear him.

"No, thanks. I'll pass," Marvin replied calmly, staring straight ahead as he tried to ignore the fact that Bo-Bo was less than a foot away from the left side of his head. Beau was so close in fact that Marvin could smell the pepperoni pizza on his breath.

"Oh, you're chicken, huh . . . Bawk, bawk, baaaawk," Bo-Bo taunted^G as he leaned in toward Marvin, who had now turned to face him because he realized the situation wasn't going to fix itself.

"I'm not chicken," insisted Marvin, trying to remain calm.

"Well, then do it, and I will if you will,"

said Beau. He was confident Marvin would back down.

"Not interested," Marvin responded as he turned away slowly in a last-ditch effort to escape the madness that was Beau 'Bo-Bo' Bradley.

"Well, your girlfriend sure will be disappointed," said Beau.

Marvin knew that Beau Bradley wouldn't stop bugging him. Even Lindsay couldn't save him from Bo-Bo's wrath^G. That's when Marvin heard a voice in his head. It was faint at first but quickly became louder and more obvious as Marvin gained awareness of its presence.

Dude, you've gotta do it or Bo-Bo will never let it go, he heard the voice in his mind say. *Besides, there's a chance you could turn out to be a hero in Lindsay's eyes.*

As Bo-Bo continued *bawking* and Marvin continued thinking, something finally gave.

"All right Beau, let's do this!" Marvin blurted out in a commanding voice. He immediately thought, *who in the world just said that!?*

But, really, Marvin knew who it was as soon as the words flew out of his mouth. It was Marvin's other Marvin. Somebody he called 'Super-Marvin.' Think of Super-Marvin as regular Marvin's alter ego[G]. Super-Marvin was foolishly brave and stepped up occasionally, typically at the worst possible times.

Geez, what a time for Super-Marvin to speak up, Marvin thought.

"Really!?" Bo-Bo said with surprise and what almost sounded like concern in his voice.

Without looking at Lindsay or Beau and without uttering another word, Marvin turned and began walking slowly and stiffly toward the diving board ladder like a zombie searching for his next meal.

"OK, well then, you first!" said Bo-Bo while following behind Marvin and resuming his annoying *bawking* sounds. He was trying to psych Marvin out because he still assumed there was no way Marvin would go through with this crazy stunt.

After all, Bo-Bo had seen many kids much older than Marvin who were too scared to jump off the high-dive. He had even seen full-grown adults make the walk-of-shame back

down the ladder after realizing how far, and frightening, the drop really was.

"Sure, I'll go first," Marvin muttered while continuing his slow trance-like march. "Might as well just get it over with."

He finally arrived at the ladder and stopped. He knew he shouldn't look up, but he just had to see how high it really was. It was much scarier than he had even imagined it would be. Marvin slowly reached out his right hand and gripped the warm steel of the handrail as he prepared to make the climb.

→ CHAPTER 5 ←
MARVIN *HITS* THE POOL

The diving board was actually 8 feet high, but to a Marvin-sized kid, 8 feet might as well have been 50 or even 100.

Marvin slowly climbed up the ladder with his skinny legs shaking as they barely hoisted him from one step to the next. He noticed a queasy[c] feeling in his stomach. At this point, Super-Marvin was long gone. There was no trace of him anywhere in regular Marvin's head. He felt like he could throw up at any moment.

He finally made it to the top.

Well, this is it, thought Marvin. *Time to meet my maker.* "It's been a good run," he mumbled to himself.

As he stepped off the top rung of the ladder onto the diving board, each leg felt like it weighed two hundred pounds. His hands clutched the side rails. They were the only thing keeping him from falling off the edge onto the hard pool deck below.

He couldn't help but notice how the people looked so small, as if he were staring down at them from atop a 10-story building.

As he continued his "walk of doom" toward the end of the board, he suddenly became aware of the chirping of birds and the heat of the sun as it warmed the back of his neck. "Geez, the sun's even hotter way up here," he whispered to himself.

As he got closer to the edge, his senses were heightened.

He could even feel the grip of the non-slip grit on the diving board scratching his feet as he walked slowly inch by inch. His legs were progressing from a slight shake to full-on breakdancing moves until he finally reached the end of the board and stopped.

He looked to his left hoping for another boost of encouragement from Lindsay and he wasn't disappointed. "You can do it Marvin!" Lindsay yelled while waving her arms overhead and hoping that Marvin could spot her in the sea of tiny onlookers.

And then it happened.

At the very moment Marvin spotted Lindsay and heard her words of encouragement, Super-Marvin took over his body again. This time it seemed like he had shown up at just the right time. Marvin felt his knees bend slightly as he prepared to make the leap of faith . . . or death!

But, as often was the case, Super-Marvin hadn't accounted for one teensy tiny issue.

You see, Marvin was much too close to the end of the board at this point, and there was something missing—A very important component of any high-dive springboard . . . *Grit!, Grip!, Grab!* or whatever you want to call it. The end of this particular diving board was as smooth as a baby's bohiney which meant it was also as slick as a sheet of ice. Just as Marvin began to jump, his right foot slipped off the edge causing him to crash down on his own bohiney, pushing the end of the springboard down. And in the world of springboards, what goes down must come back up! The diving board spring let out a bellowing boooiiiinnng as it launched Marvin at least five feet in the air.

"Whaaaaaooooooo!!" Marvin belted out at the top of his lungs as he plummeted toward his impending doom at what seemed like 100 miles per hour.

WHACK! Marvin hit the water in a half dive, half belly flop, V-shaped jackknife^G position,

which immediately knocked the wind out of him and shot him toward the bottom of the pool like a missile.

"Oooouuuuuch!" he yelled while still submerged deep below the water's surface.

Marvin struggled his way back to the top as quickly as he could. It seemed like it had taken forever to reach the surface. He was in shock and gasping for air, but he felt lucky to be alive.

However, he was even more shocked, and confused, by what awaited him.

Rather than boos, ridicule or harassment, Marvin was greeted with the clapping and cheers of every single person at the pool.

Wow! Marvin thought upon seeing all the clapping kids, *I think I just dove into the pool from the high dive. I'm going to be a hero!*

I am a total hero! he thought once again.

The panic he had just been feeling now quickly turned into something else, and that something else was ELATION! Marvin managed to get one hand up out of the water to give a cool and calm thumbs up to the crowd, or "fans" as he would now think of them.

But then Marvin became aware of another feeling besides elation[G]. It was a strange sensation of freedom. He couldn't recall

having had that freedom-feeling when he was in the pool earlier.

"Marvin! Your swim trunks!" He heard Lindsay's kind voice loudly whisper from the side of the pool.

"They're behind you!" she continued.

Yep, he was free alright . . . free of the swimsuit he'd had on just seconds earlier when he was freefalling from the high dive.

"Oh, man!" Marvin exclaimed as he scrambled to push the trunks under water and get his legs through the holes.

Marvin still wasn't sure exactly what had just happened or how exactly he had managed to lose his swimsuit, but he did know one thing, everyone was chanting one phrase loud and proud.

"Maaarvin!, Maaarvin!, Maaarvin!" the crowd called as if they were rooting on their favorite athlete in an Olympic event.

Even the people who didn't know Marvin had joined in on the action . . . "Maaarvin! Maaarvin!" they continued.

As Marvin doggy-paddled his way to the edge of the pool, Lindsay was waiting for him with an open hand to help him out.

"Wow, Marvin you are one brave boy," Lindsay said with a gleam in her eye. Then, she immediately turned to Beau Bradley.

"Looks like you're up Booo-Booo!" she said loudly while staring Beau directly in the eyes.

You can imagine the look on Beau's face after what he had just seen. He looked confused and scared all at the same time.

Nobody knew it, but Beau had never jumped off the high-dive board. Frankly, he had been banking on the fact that Marvin would chicken out, which would mean he would be off the hook.

Thanks to Super-Marvin, that plan was all washed up.

"I think I'll pass," said Beau, still petrified^G by the death-defying feat he had just witnessed. So much so in fact, that he hadn't even noticed Lindsay calling him by his nickname.

"Yeah, it takes a mighty brave kid to do what Marvin just did," Lindsay said as she continued staring down Beau who was already walking away slowly as if nothing had even happened.

Still holding Marvin's hand, Lindsay walked him toward the birthday area. "Will you help me open a few of my gifts?" she asked. "I might need some extra muscle to help tear open the boxes."

"You bet!" Marvin whispered to her, still in a daze from the trauma he had just endured, "... but first, let me run to the bathroom and turn my swim trunks around the right way. I think I'll tie them this time too."

"Good idea, Marvin, I'll wait for you right here," Lindsay said as she let go of his hand with a giggle and a smile.

→ LESSON ←

Sometimes in life you will just have
to be brave. But, who knows, you
just might end up being a hero.

→ GLOSSARY ←

ALTER EGO A different personality or different self but still inside your same self so it's like two *selfs* in one. Well, never mind, just learn this one later. I'm tired of explaining it and I still have a lot of words to define.

CONFISCATE To take away. If I confiscate your ice cream cone you will not be happy.

DIFFUSE To take the element of 'explosion' out of something. If your mom is yelling "For the one-millionth time, please just clean your room!!" you can diffuse her frustration and anger by cleaning your room. It's simple, right?

ELATION   Feeling excited.

HURRIEDLY   Trying to do something in a hurry which you always do when you are about to go do something you want to do. Otherwise, you do it Slowly. Go ahead ask your parents. It's true.

INTIMIDATING   Scary, but not like a scary movie scary. It's more like somebody being mean to you type scary. Don't be intimidating. Be kind.

JACKKNIFE   An old school term for *pocketknife* but it's also a type of *dive* where you look like a half-opened pocketknife.

LOOMING   Imminent, Impending— Well, I'm not really sure what it means, but it's a cool sounding word so I used it. If you find out send me a message.

PETRIFIED   Scared out of your mind. If you had to the spend the night in a graveyard you would be PETRIFIED!

PLUMMETED To fall quickly (never fun unless into a foam pit!).

PLUNGED The act of jumping or diving into the water.

QUEASY When you feel like you are going to blow chunks (you know, barf! vomit! spew! hurl!).

STOIC Maintaining calmness and control in a time of distress. For example, if you were being bullied by some bully you should try to control your emotions and remain stoic. Well, or freak out and run!

SWIMMINGLY Going well or going smoothly. I only used it because the root of the word is swim. This story is probably the first time I have used the word in like ten years.

TAUNT   It's when you bug or even insult someone. Don't do it. It's not cool. Spend time building your friends up with comments like "You Are Awesome!"

WRATH   Anger or rage. See the definition of *Diffuse* and read the part about the mom.

Made in the USA
Lexington, KY
18 February 2019